To my friend
Kay

Captain Hans Harms

Ballad of the RagMan

Written by Cynthia Blomquist Gustavson

Illustrated by Kristina Tosic

blooming twig books

Blooming Twig Books / New York

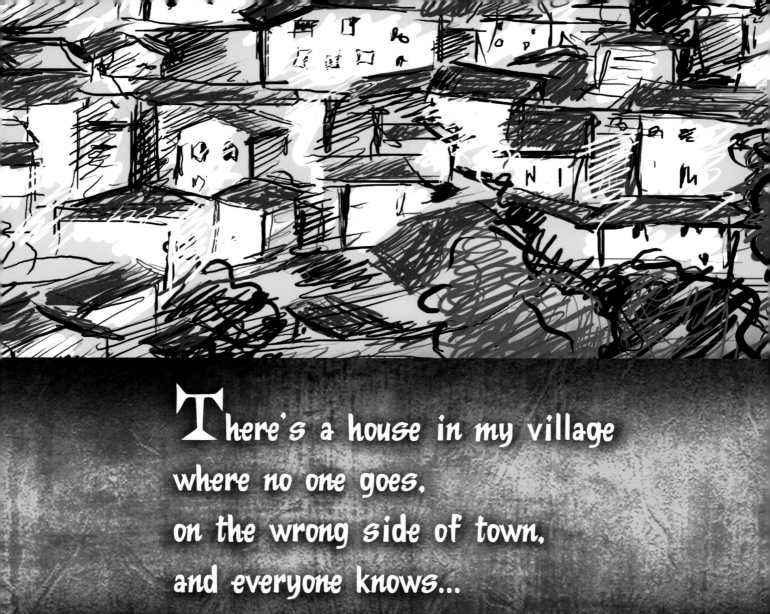

There's a house in my village
where no one goes,
on the wrong side of town,
and everyone knows...

The yard is a dump
full of everything old,
a dangerous place
for children, I'm told

It's the rag man's house,
where he lives alone
collecting old things
neighbors have thrown.

Such as cuckoo clocks
with doors ajar,
and dozens of buckets
coated with tar.

Sofa pillows
and parts of cars,
refrigerators, ovens
and iron bars,

Mattresses
with rusty springs,
boxes, boards.

And airplane wings,
the real things!

Before the garbage truck has come,
he pushes his cart by every home.

And sifts through trash
piled in a heap,
deciding which junk
he wants to keep.

He took my broken rocking chair, and my faded, eyeless teddy bear.

And the neighbor's swing, mostly rust,
plus a smoke detector they couldn't trust.

And paint cans full of drips of color, and their lumpy sofa faded duller... than my t-shirt with the flying heart, and he heaped them high on his rusty cart...

Then wheeled it away to who-knows-where.
But what did he do with my teddy bear?
I didn't want him left in a barrel somewhere.

I followed behind so he wouldn't see,
and hid behind an old oak tree.

He rolled his cart into a back shed door,
shut tight - so I could see no more.

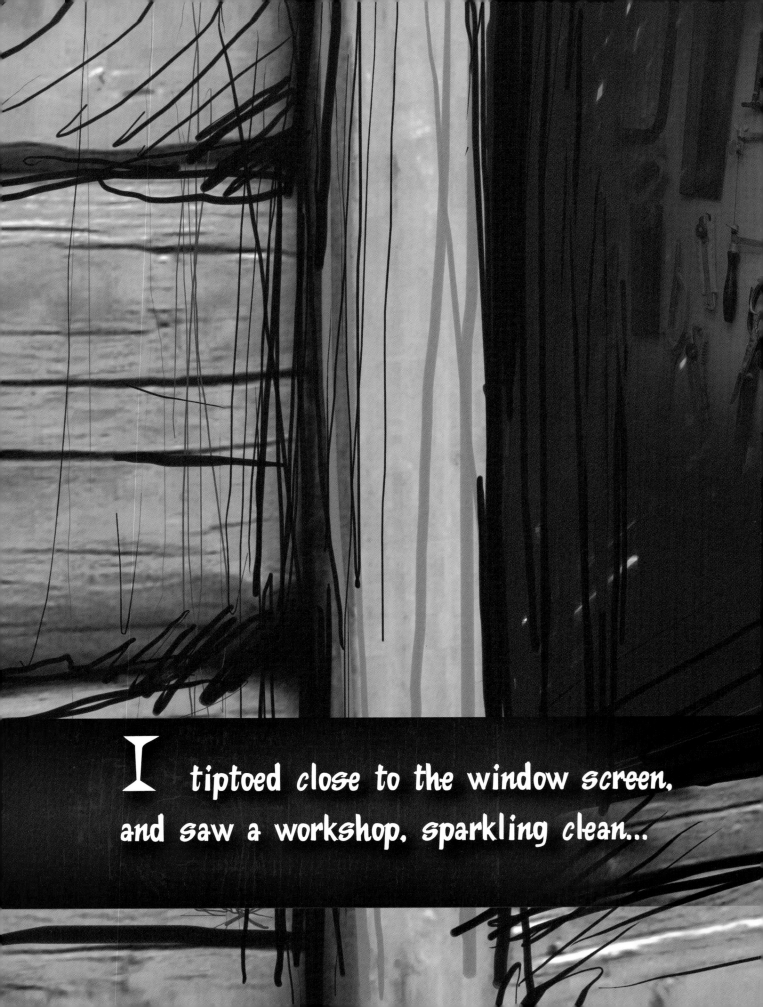

I tiptoed close to the window screen, and saw a workshop, sparkling clean...

Where old clocks ticked and rockers rocked, records spun and lockets locked.

Then I saw the rag man
ease from his cart
my broken-down teddy
and hold it to his heart.

He dusted its head and washed its fur,
sewed an eye gently, as if it were
something more precious than silver or gold,
something a little child would yearn to hold.

I ran back home, fast as the wind,
too scared to tell anyone where I'd been.

All fixed up fine, with fur so clean,
the finest teddy I'd ever seen.

The night was long,
but dreams were sweet.

And when I awoke,
there at my feet...

Looking brand new,
with fur so neat,

Lay the teddy bear
I'd seen the rag man fix!

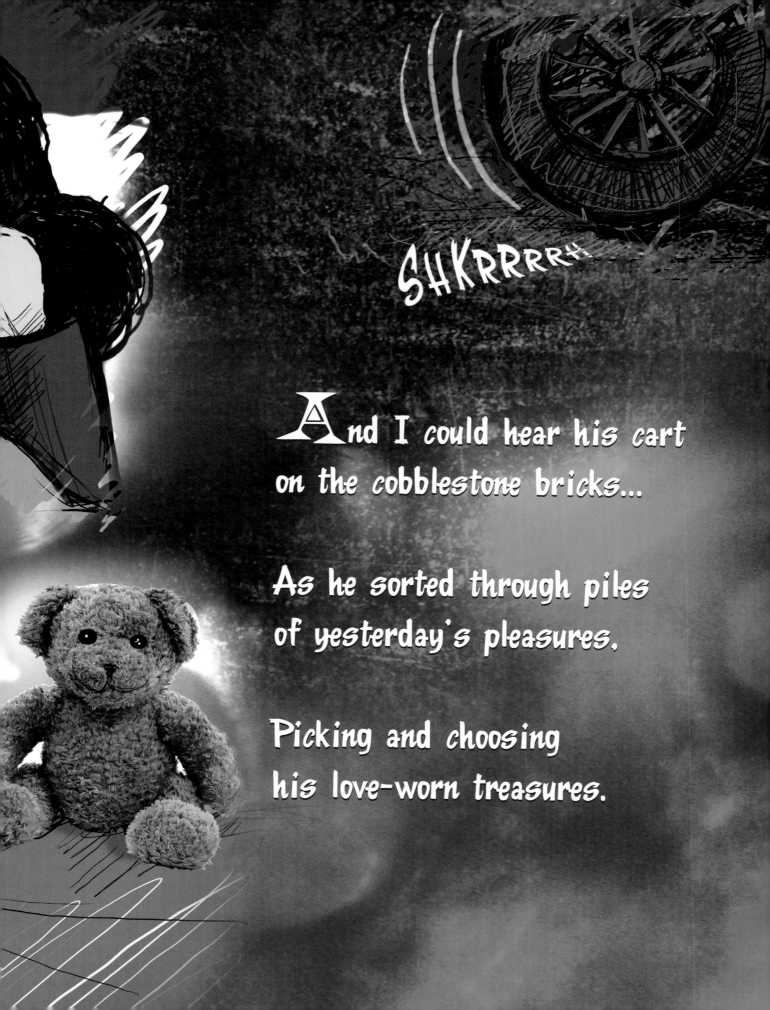

SHKRRRR+!

And I could hear his cart
on the cobblestone bricks...

As he sorted through piles
of yesterday's pleasures,

Picking and choosing
his love-worn treasures.

I looked out the window, and smiled down the street.

Thanking the rag man
for the gift at my feet.

I will hug my teddy for the rest of his days,
and never again fear the rag man's ways.

"To Daniel, the strangest and kindest man I ever knew."
— C.B.G.

"To my mother."
— K.T.

www.bloomingtwigbooks.com

Gustavson, Cynthia Blomquist.
Ballad of the Rag Man / written by Cynthia Blomquist Gustavson ;
illustrated by Kristina Tosic. p. cm.
Summary: The Rag Man collects cast-off items. A little girl watches from a distance as he takes her old teddy bear, and follows him to his mysterious shop. To her surprise, the Rag Man repairs her teddy bear...
ISBN 978-1-933918-42-6

First Edition / First Printing
10 9 8 7 6 5 4 3 2 1

Blooming Twig Books LLC
PO Box 4668 #66675
New York, NY 10163-4668
1-866-389-1482